Grandma Rose

Emkay McAllister

For Grandmas and Grandpas everywhere

I love you
Nana Freda
Grandpa Don
Grandpa Rex
Grandma Teri

CONTENTS

A note from Grandma Rose –

This is my heart-felt, heart-warming tale about looking at life through a lens of contentment.
My message and plea from me to you: Enjoy and strive for contentment in all the days of your beautiful life.

the beginning

Move-in day was the day before Violet's birthday. The only proof that there was a birthday girl in the house was a piece of chocolate cake in the otherwise bare fridge.

"Violet, sweetie-pie?"

"Yes, Mama?" Violet Sweetie-Pie said sweetly.

"I want to talk to you about something."

Am I in trouble? I can't be in trouble the day before my birthday, said Violet's thoughts. "What?" she said instead.

"Come sit on Mama's lap."

Eight-year-old-about-to-turn-nine-year-old Violet sat on her mama's lap.

Mama had a pretty smile on her face. "There is a nice old lady who lives across the street from us. Her name is Grandma Rose and I wanted to ask you if you want to go visit her sometimes."

Violet's eyes were wide, dramatic. "But old people can be scary."

Mama laughed her pretty laugh, then said, "Violet, you loved your Grandma Teri and your Papa Donald and your Nana Freda. And you love your Grandpa Rex."

Now Violet was giggling. "They're not scary," she decided.

After a shake of her head, Mama told her daughter, "I promise that Grandma Rose isn't scary either." And then: "Let's you and me go meet her today after we unpack some things."

The social anxiety in Violet was overcome with an instant excitement. "Okay. Can we give her cookies?" Violet hoped. Cookies for this Grandma Rose lady meant cookies for her!

"If I can find the flour," Mama laughed, again, that pretty Mama laugh.

*****

The next day, Mama was able to find the flour. The smell of Mama's nostalgic chocolate-chip cookies were comforting after the stress of moving.

Violet and Mama wouldn't get to see the magic that lived within Grandma Rose's house that day.

There was a little old lady outside the little old house rocking in a sunny-yellow rocking chair. The rocking chair had little smiley-face stickers all over it which Violet recognized to belong to Walmart; sometimes the nice old people at Walmart stuck the smiley stickers on kids' hands when they either came into or left the store. Violet thought about the nice old people at Walmart. *Well, if someone gave you a smiley-face sticker, doesn't that mean they're nice?* Violet thought.

The little old lady who must certainly be Grandma Rose had a Walmart-sticker-smile written on her face.

Mama was the first of the three on the porch to say something. "Hi there. You must be the kind woman they call Grandma Rose. We just moved in and wanted to introduce ourselves. I'm Meadow Graves and this is my daughter, Violet."

The old woman's smile grew. "What a sunny day, meeting new friends."

Violet frowned. The day wasn't sunny at all. It looked like rain to her.

Mama gave a sunny smile though. "We were making some cookies and we thought of you, Miss Rose."

No, that's not what happened, Mama. We thought of her and then *made some cookies,* Violet thought to herself.

Then she corrected that thought: *We thought of her and* then *made some cookies… because I wanted some.*

The old woman rose from her rocking chair to accept the cookies. "There's no Miss Rose here. Please, call me Grandma Rose."

Mama smiled her famous smile. "Alright then, Grandma Rose."

Violet gave the old woman a polite but hesitant smile. She received an animated wink in return.

And that was the end of Violet's first visit to see Grandma Rose.

On the walk back home which was just across the street, Violet's wide and curious eyes hungrily absorbed the scene around her. The little girl had been too nervous to pay much attention to her surroundings on the way to meet Grandma Rose.

There were pink flamingoes in Grandma Rose's yard. Violet counted them to find that there was an odd number of eleven. Violet started walking backwards so that her eyes could still linger and enjoy Grandma Rose's mad property. While doing her little backward walk, her eyes discovered a lone plastic cow that matched the style of the flamingoes.

There was a sign to the right of the black-and-white cow that told people to "be patient and loving and don't have a cow." That started Violet laughing. Mama started laughing because Violet was laughing. Then Mama asked her what was so funny. Violet's response? "Don't have a cow, Mama. I'm only laughing." That just made Mama throw her head back and laugh a little louder and a little harder.

"Don't have a cow" was Grandpa Rex's most common phrase and believing that Grandma Rose liked the phrase, too, was what got Violet smiling and laughing.

Grandma Rose

After a light knock at the green door which Violet thought to be not a pretty green, Violet was let into the little old house by the little old lady named Grandma Rose.

"Violet Graves. Hello, hello, hello. Welcome, welcome, welcome." Grandma Rose was of a warm, quirky personality. And there was a strangeness in her that no one could name. It was an undefined mystery.

Violet's eyes admired the sight. Streamers of every color were attached to every corner of the ceiling in Violet's view.

Violet was curious. "Whose birthday is it?"

Grandma Rose was smiling. "Well, I heard that yesterday was yours."

How did Grandma Rose know that? Now Violet was very curious. "You did all this… for me?"

"Well, I do this for everyone. Every day is someone's birthday. And every day should be a party." Grandma Rose liked winking.

"Do you ever take it down?" Violet wanted to know.

"No," Grandma Rose chuckled. "But they do seem to fall down on their own sometimes."

Violet looked at the creaky floor she was walking on. Yellow floorboards. The wooden floor was painted *yellow.*

The inquisitive girl half-frowned and half-smiled. "I've never seen a yellow floor in a house before."

"Yes, well, I like to walk on sunshine." Another wink followed the words.

As soon as Grandma Rose finished her sentence, there was a frantic, frenzied pitter-patter quickly approaching.

"Wiener dogs!" Violet squealed when she saw two little dachshunds race from the kitchen.

Petting the colorful spotted one, she asked, "What's this one's name?"

Grandma Rose smiled. "Daxton."

Then Violet pointed to the shaggy brown one, asking, "What's that one's name?"

"Daxton." Grandma Rose's smile had widened.

Unlike Grandma Rose, Violet wasn't smiling. "They're both named Daxton?"

"Yes," Grandma Rose giggled.

Violet's confusion and curiosity continued. "Why do they have the same name?"

After a shrug and a pause, Grandma Rose said lightly, "Why not?"

Grandma Rose noticed that something in Violet's wide eyes wanted more information than that. And so she decided to explain. "I love the name Daxton. All the dogs I've ever had have been named Daxton. And I have used the same dog bowls since my first dog. Both the food dish and the water dish have DAXTON engraved on them. So that means I never need to buy more dog bowls."

With a tilt of her head, Violet could only say "Oh."

"I'm a crazy dog lady." Grandma Rose winked.

Will she ever stop winking?

Quite matter-of-factly, Violet said, "My mama asked me to ask you to tell me a little bit about yourself."

The words came out in a voice of awe. "Well, I wake up at 3 every morning to enjoy the stars when nobody else does."

Violet looked at Grandma Rose with a funny expression and she could have sworn that she was looking at stars in Grandma Rose's eyes.

Now the question was turned and Grandma Rose said, "If it's okay, I want to ask you to tell me a little bit about yourself."

"What do you want to know? I'm an open book. That's what people tell me." The little girl was still matter-of-fact, though her face was turning red from all the attention and the very direct question.

"What is your favorite color?"

"That's easy. Purple," Violet announced.

"Ah. Purple," Grandma Rose approved. "Why purple?"

Violet sighed, thinking, before explaining, "It matches my name. Violets are kind of purple-y."

"So your favorite color is purple," Grandma Rose mused. "That must mean that you know you are a princess. Purple is a royal color. The color of royalty."

There was a quiet between them, both thinking and in their own worlds.

"What is your favorite color?" asked Violet of Grandma Rose.

A Grandma Rose smile and wink. "The rainbow."

"The rainbow?" Violet repeated in question.

"I like all the colors. They are all my favorite. All the colors make me happy. They make me smile." And Grandma Rose was smiling.

The conversation continued for over an hour, flowing easily, made up of many questions and answers.

Finally peeking at the clock – more like wincing – Violet slowly said, "I'm sorry, but Mama wants me home for dinner. I have to go, Miss…? Umm. What should I call you?" Violet's mind went blank.

"Grandma Rose. Everybody calls me Grandma Rose."

She looked like a Grandma Rose.

"Okay, Grandma Rose. It's time for me to go home now." Violet didn't know her new house very well yet, but she already decided that she liked Grandma Rose's house more.

Grandma Rose gave a big grandma hug.

"Roses are red…" she sang.

"Violets are blue…" she continued.

"Today was a fun day with you!" she finished.

Violet smiled shyly.

Just when Violet was ready to close the door after her, Grandma Rose called out from her spot on the couch. "Oh Violet, come over again tomorrow and I'll have a late birthday present waiting for you."

Violet nodded, smiled, and promised she would.

Violet decided that day that Grandma Rose was a mysterious, magical old lady. And that she already loved her like a grandma.

*****

It was the next day and Violet found herself knocking at Grandma Rose's front door at 6 a.m., still in her pajamas. Her purple butterfly pajamas.

"Violet." There was no surprise or shock in her voice; Grandma Rose was humored, not fazed. "Come in, come in. Does your mama know you're here?"

"I left a note" seemed enough of an explanation to little Violet.

Grandma Rose was checking for further information. "Ah, a note. What did your note say?"

The little girl shrugged, shrugging off the question as well. "It said that I want to hang out with Grandma Rose."

Smiling, Grandma Rose asked Violet, "What do you usually eat for breakfast?"

"What do *you* usually eat for breakfast?" Violet asked the question right back. Grandma Rose had more fun things to say than anyone little Violet ever knew; Violet's answer wouldn't be nearly as interesting, Violet was sure.

"Dessert. Candy. Sweets. Sugar."

"Your mama lets you?" Then Violet remembered; grandmas usually don't have mamas anymore.

Smiling sadly, Grandma Rose said, "Old grannies like me don't have mamas anymore." Violet knew that. "But my mama was quite the little baker and I have one sugary treat every morning in honor of her."

Violet imagined the scene Grandma Rose described. "You must have been a very good daughter."

Grandma Rose smiled. "Now, what would you like for breakfast? I can bake anything you'd like."

Violet followed Grandma Rose further into the house and into the kitchen. There was a giant kitchen table in the dining area. Paint splatters of every color of the rainbow decorated the entire table. Each chair was a different shade of yellow and was its own unique style. Violet counted twelve chairs. As she was counting, she was thinking to herself, *How are there that many yellows?* (shades of yellow)

Grandma Rose was silent as Violet counted up the chairs.

Finished counting, Violet assumed, "Do you have a big family?"

"No, just me, just old Grandma Rose," the old woman said quickly. Too quickly.

Violet thought about that for a moment. "Why do you have such a big table and so many chairs?"

"Why not?" Grandma Rose winked mysteriously. Then she added, "I never sit in the same chair more than two days in a row."

Soon enough, Grandma Rose and Violet were splitting a small chocolate cake.

"I had chocolate cake for my birthday," Violet said proudly, sharing her good news.

"And you and your mama brought me chocolate-chip cookies," Grandma Rose noted. "You must love chocolate."

Violet clasped her hands together. "I love chocolate."

The little chocolate cake was already nearly gobbled up; it was having a quick death.

"This is like Thanksgiving! Good food, big table, lots of chairs, fun," Violet said through teeth covered in chocolate cake. "We just need a turkey and more people."

Grandma Rose smiled with sad eyes. And Violet commented on them. "Are you crying?"

One lone tear fell from Grandma Rose's glistening eye and into her piece of cake. "Yes, my eyes are crying and I don't know why."

With an animated tilt of her head, Violet said in a most serious tone, "Well, your eyes won't tell you why you're crying. They're just eyes."

Grandma Rose started laughing. Her laughter brought new tears, these ones fresh and happy.

*****

The rest of the day involved laughter and included Grandma Rose Happy Tears. Violet would never know that Grandma Rose was having a very hard day that day. But she would forever be grateful and indebted for that beautiful day.

*****

So what was the present to Violet from Grandma Rose? A set of mittens. Small like Violet's hands.

Christmas every day

There it was. It was decorated so extremely that you almost couldn't tell what on earth it was.

"I didn't know you had a Christmas tree," Violet said in wonder. "Christmas in the summer?"

Grandma Rose motioned for Violet to come closer to get a better look at it. "It stays up all year."

"*All* year?" Violet emphasized, slowly walking over to the tree.

Grandma Rose explained. "Every time I have a new guest in my house, they get to leave with a present. They get to pick a gift under the tree."

Violet was hesitant but too curious not to ask. "Do I get a present, too?"

Grandma Rose smiled warmly. "You're a guest, aren't you?"

Violet shrugged, then nodded.

After a light sigh, Grandma Rose said, "But I should tell you…"

"Tell me what?" Violet asked, still curious, always curious.

Grandma Rose's face was serious. "I should tell you that I won't be able to give you a present *every* time you come over." Then her face became light and bright again.

"I have a feeling that you'll come over to my house quite a bit."

Violet had to smile when Grandma Rose smiled. "Well, I like you."

"I like you, too, Violet," Grandma Rose said, then, "I hope you understand about the presents. It's just Grandma Rose won't be able to have enough presents to go around if someone gets a present every day."

"Does that mean I can come over every day?" Violet asked, hopeful.

"My door is always open," Grandma Rose told her.

Violet shook her head quickly. "That's not a good idea. Mama and me used to leave the door open when it was nice outside and lots of flies got in the house."

Grandma Rose laughed. She was still laughing as she went down the narrow hallway, leaving Violet confused and wondering. But the little old lady came back holding a little cutely-wrapped present. It was cutely-wrapped because it wasn't wrapped well at all.

Grandma Rose was giggling mischievously when she said, "Now this, Violet, is *your* gift. I feel very good about this gift."

Violet was invited to open her present. It was a box. In a box. In a box. Finally Violet got down to the real box.

She carefully and cautiously opened the small little thing. Inside was… a rock. Violet's eyes squinted and her forehead wrinkled in thought.

"Are you sure you want to give me this?" Violet said, raising her eyebrows.

Grandma Rose smiled and winked at the same time. "Oh don't worry, I have plenty."

Violet was shaking her head again. "But it's a rock."

"It is, yes. But a rock can be a lot of things. Where did it come from? How did it get here? What does it do? What can you do with a rock?"

Violet shrugged, still puzzled. "You can skip a rock… You can paint a rock… You can kick a rock."

First an approving nod, then a sorrowful shake of the head, Grandma Rose said, "Life is like a rock, Violet. Remember that."

Now Violet was tilting her head and squinting her eyes again. "Remember what?"

Violet wouldn't understand until she was much older why Grandma Rose's voice was so melancholy when she said the words: "For now, I want you to remember that life may be simple and everyday and sometimes small. But it can be a lot of things."

Violet sighed, confused still.

The sudden ticking of the lone clock on the wall made Violet jump which made Grandma Rose laugh.

Violet frowned. "Dinner-time. I have to go. Bye, Grandma Rose."

Violet extended her hand, wanting a handshake. Grandma Rose took it with one hand and patted it with the other.

The old woman's face was rarely this serious. "Don't forget your rock. And try to remember what I told you about it."

With a shrug, Violet told her, "I'm still kind of confused, but thank you."

When Violet got home, she hurried up the stairs and into her room and put her new rock in her blue treasure chest under her bed.

lonely by yourself

"Grandma Rose? I have a question." Violet's voice was down.

Grandma Rose liked questions. "I'll try to answer your question honestly," she said.

"Do you want to get married?" Violet blurted out the question in rushed bravery.

"Do I want to get married?" Grandma Rose repeated the question to herself.

Violet tried another question. "Have you ever been married before?"

The old woman's eyes looked different than usual in this moment. "No, Grandma Rose has never been married before."

Violet hesitated on the question, then chose to ask anyway. "Have you ever been in love before?"

"I think everyone will become in love with someone sometime in their lifetime," was the old woman's perspective.

The expression on Violet's face told Grandma Rose that she wanted more than that. So Grandma Rose gave it to her.

"Yes, I was in love. I was in love with a boy named Skye. We were young and he wanted to marry me. Then he died. And I have never been in love with anyone else." Her voice was so unlike Grandma Rose as she said the words.

"Oh" was the only noise that Violet could make.

Grandma Rose had lost her smile. "Why are you asking Grandma Rose these questions?"

The words were blurted out: "I was wondering if you want to marry my Grandpa Rex."

A smile flickered and went out on Grandma Rose's lips. "Thank you for wondering a beautiful thought like that. But Grandma Rose likes being alone."

Violet said "Oh" again.

"Is your Grandpa Rex lonely?" Grandma Rose asked Violet.

Violet shook her head before she gave her answer. "No. I asked him that question the last time I saw him and he said that he likes being alone, too."

Grandma Rose smiled down at her hands folded in her lap. Violet wondered when the last time was that Grandma Rose's hands were intertwined with another's. She was almost tempted to reach out and hold her hand.

"Are you lonely? Or are you just alone?" Her voice was quietly concerned.

The answer? "I am Grandma Rose. And Grandma Rose doesn't mind being alone. You can't feel lonely if you're a little crazy – you have to make things fun and you have to do it yourself. You can't rely on other people for the fun because people come and people go and you are stuck with yourself all day and all night, so you might as well learn to make things fun."

Violet would never forget the speech and she would paraphrase it throughout her life to ears that needed to hear it.

park days

Grandma Rose recommended to Violet and Mama that they go to the park every once in a while to feed the birds; it didn't matter the season or your mood. Mama decided that today, a random Thursday, was a good day to start the new family tradition. On the way home, Violet asked a question and started a sad conversation.

"How did Grandpa Don die?"

Mama looked back at her daughter through the car rear-view mirror. "He had a disease called Parkinson's."

"And it killed him?" Violet wanted clarification.

Mama nodded. "Yes, it did."

Violet shook her head. "That makes me sad." There was a moment of silence, then Violet said, "I don't want Grandma Rose to die."

"Everyone will die, Violet. It's a part of life. It's just what happens. We don't know when we're going to die, but we will all die one day." They were sad words said in a sad voice.

"I know," Violet said quietly. "I just don't want Grandma Rose to die."

"Then we should enjoy the time we get to spend with her. Right?" Mama briefly looked back at the backseat to look into her daughter's face. Mama tried a smile for her daughter's sake.

"Right. That sounds good." The little girl's voice was still sorrowful, like she had already lost her Grandma Rose.

*****

Violet knew that she would be very sad and very lonely without Grandma Rose when Grandma Rose left her for heaven. She wouldn't sleep well the next several nights and one of the reasons for the insomnia was the fear of Grandma Rose one day leaving this world.

Fishing

"Ready for today's adventure?"

"I'm already excited about tomorrow's," Violet commented.

Grandma Rose could have jumped up and down, she was so excited.

"So, Grandma Rose, what is it?" Violet pressed, trying and failing to be patient.

After a suspenseful pause, Grandma Rose said with utmost pride, "I talked to your mama and she allowed it."

Violet's smile widened. She knew this was going to be a good day if Mama had to allow something.

"We're going fishing!" Grandma Rose almost yelled.

Fishing? Violet's excitement and curiosity was swiftly dying. "Fishing? But I've never been fishing. I don't know how. I'll be bad."

The wink was there with the words: "Oh you'll like this fishing."

Violet sniffed the backyard air and it was so chilly and fresh that it almost stung her nose. "Why are we fishing when it's fall? It won't be a nice sunny day."

"We'll make it sunny with our sunny personalities." A smile and yet another wink.

Violet noticed that Grandma Rose never drove. Violet enjoyed their short walk to the surprise destination which she soon discovered was a pond in a fenceless field.

Grandma Rose reached into her grandma bag and withdrew… *leaves.* Autumn leaves. Some golden, others brown, others red, others orange. Violet's immediate favorite was a green leaf turning yellow.

"Now, Violet. This is a lesson, an activity. No, an *adventure.*" It was almost a warning, a teasing warning at that. Grandma Rose's voice was saying, *You better pay attention because this is going to be fun.*

Dead leaves? Fun? Violet thought, then said, "What do a bunch of dead leaves have to do with fishing?"

"Well, I'll tell you," Grandma Rose said, "Do you know that this life is all about fishing?"

Violet slowly and unsurely shook her head. "I didn't know that."

Grandma Rose nodded a 'yes.' "In life, Violet, we are fishing for all kinds of things. We try to catch the best fish. The best memories and experiences. We want to catch true love and we want to catch our dreams. We try to find the best catch."

Violet's confusion was evident on her face. "Okay."

"What are some of your dreams, Violet?" the question was.

Violet smiled at the thought. "I want to be like my mama."

"Don't you want to be like Violet?" Grandma Rose asked the girl.

Violet had some questions herself. "Grandma Rose, what does it mean to be yourself? How can you do that? I don't know who I am yet."

Grandma Rose winked. "But that is the magic of it all."

Violet almost winked back in good humor, but she didn't want to embarrass herself; she had never winked before and thought she would probably be bad at it.

Grandma Rose wanted something further. "Now. What are some other dreams that you have?"

"I want a puppy." Violet's eyes sparkled, her mind imagining furry paws and wagging tails.

"What else?" Grandma Rose pushed.

A pause filled the air.

Then: "Have you ever thought about what you want to be when you grow up?"

"A teacher," Violet said, her voice sounding dreamy.

And then: "Have you ever thought about getting married or having kids?"

Violet turned the question. "Have you? Is that your dream? Was it?"

Sadness glittered in Grandma Rose's eyes. "Maybe a long time ago. But dreams change. If we want them to." The silence welcomed a long thoughtful pause. Elderly woman and young lady stared out into the open pond.

Then Grandma Rose summarized, concluding, "So you want to be a good person like your mama. And you want to be a teacher, too. And you also want a puppy. And maybe have a family someday?"

"Yes, but that dream might change like yours did," Violet supposed.

Grandma Rose briefly looked at Violet, then her gaze went back to the happy pond. "Do you think your dream to have a family will change?"

Violet blinked, then squinted in thought. "Did you think yours would?"

Her tone was grief. "As soon as he died, yes. Yes, that dream died the day he died."

That upset-Grandma-Rose voice made Violet's heart hurt. So Violet was grateful for the next comment that lightened the heavy air.

"Now, I have a pack of Goldfish with me here…"
Then appeared a small pack of Goldfish crackers. "…And
each one of the little Goldfish inside represents one of your
dreams. Don't eat the Goldfish. Keep them in their bag and
leave them with the leaves."

Violet could only blink.

"And now, the leaves… I want you to take them
and leave them in this shoebox and add in four flowers and
a four-leaf clover when the weather changes and gets
warm." Then Grandma Rose mused, "Dying leaves, dying
dreams, to be born again in green."

When Violet didn't say anything, that was when
Grandma Rose's smile grew bigger in its humor. "Any
questions?"

"Why?" was all Violet could say to that.

"Why?" Grandma Rose laughed loudly. "Why do
we do anything?"

Violet said it with uncertainty: "Because we want
to?"

Violet never saw Grandma Rose tilt her head like
that before. "Do you want your dreams to come true,
Violet?" the old woman asked the young girl.

The young girl's eyes danced with imagination.
"Yes."

"Then you have to catch those dreams!" It was almost a cheer.

Violet wanted to know, "How?"

Grandma Rose knew. "Well, you have a pond. And in that pond are many fish called *Dreams*. You must feed each Dream fish well so that it will grow into a beautiful dream. And then when that fish is big enough and when that dream is dreamed up enough, you catch that Dream fish! And that's when your dream will come true."

"So how do I feed my Dream fish?" Violet was curious to know.

So Grandma Rose told her. "You keep dreaming. You keep dreaming, Violet, and you do all the steps that will lead you to your dream."

There were many sunny dreams in Violet's eyes, Grandma Rose could tell.

Then Grandma Rose gave the example, "If you want to be like your mama, you need to spend time with her and get to know her better. You can't truly admire someone until you know them."

Now there was a deep admiration in Violet's eyes.

"And you said you want to be a teacher, too, is that right?" Grandma Rose wanted to confirm.

Violet nodded.

"Then what do you think you ought to do?"
Grandma Rose asked.

Violet knew, but didn't necessarily like the fact. "I have to do good in school."

"You mean you have to do *well* in school," Grandma Rose corrected.

Violet's mind went to memories of and experiences in school, nice teachers and mean girls and bad grades.

Grandma Rose soon got Violet's mind thinking on other things though. "And there was something else on your list… What was it, a puppy?"

"Yeah." Violet's big eyes reminded Grandma Rose of a puppy-dog's eyes in that moment.

"Then there are several things you could do," Grandma Rose helped. "You could pet-sit. You could walk dogs. You could go the pet store and decide what kind of puppy you want in the future."

Violet really liked puppies. It was a good dream.

Dreaming was very important to Grandma Rose. "Think about those dreams often, Violet. Know it's okay to change your mind about them. Know that it's always possible to reach them. Dream, please don't forget to dream. Dream and catch those fish."

Violet did this challenge.

*****

One day, if you visited Miss Violet's third grade classroom, you would find the words on the wall:

To all the dreamers (and I hope that's all of you)…

Dream and hope and wish

Go to your dream pond

Each dream lives in each fish

Catch your dreams

Sometimes it seems

Life is too hard

Too short

But still cast your line

And soon you'll be able to say

"That dream is mine."

tick-tock of time

Violet stared at the clocks staring at her. "Grandma Rose?" she called out.

"Yes, Violet?" Then Grandma Rose was standing beside the girl, also staring at the clocks tick-tocking on the wall. Grandma Rose's staring was in wonder and Violet's staring was in confusion.

"I have a question…" Violet started.

Grandma Rose smiled, her eyes still on the faces of the clocks. "I would be happy to answer."

Violet frowned. "These clocks. Are they new?"

"They are new," Grandma Rose validated.

Violet found that a strange fact. "Don't you think a new clock would tell the right time?"

"Oh Violet, I took out all the batteries." Grandma Rose's smile was turning into an almost-smirk.

"Why would you do that?" Violet was clearly mystified.

"There is no time," was the confusing answer.

Violet didn't smile. "Well, aren't you late to places?"

"I like to be early actually," Grandma Rose said.

"How can you be early if you don't know the time?" Violet was anxious to know.

Grandma Rose put her hand over her heart. Violet immediately noticed the blue wristwatch on her itty-bitty, teeny-tiny wrist.

"I keep the real time close to my heart." Then the woman winked. "I keep the good times close to my heart."

Violet's eyes left Grandma Rose's winking eye to look at the clocks again. "Broken clocks," Violet whispered. "Huh."

"Yes," was all Grandma Rose said.

a storm in the soul

"Grandma Rose," Violet whispered frantically, her voice slightly panicked.

The old woman lay silent and peaceful in her little twin-sized bed, eyes closed, breathing steady.

"Grandma Rose… you're awake?" the little girl voice said.

Grandma Rose's voice, "Of course I'm awake. It's 3 a.m." Then, "Why are you awake?"

Violet explained simply, "The storm."

Eyes now open, still steady-breathing and in a steady voice, Grandma Rose asked, "Does your mama know you're here?"

"I left a note." Now Violet had a question to ask: "Why is your door unlocked?"

Grandma Rose's answer: "In case little girls afraid of storms come over to my house."

Violet was learning that Grandma Rose's winks meant that she was just joking or saying something really bizarre. This happened often.

Then Violet asked of Grandma Rose, "Can I watch the stars with you?"

"Oh, there's no stars out tonight. And we wouldn't be able to enjoy them if they were," Grandma Rose described.

Violet was frowning, but Grandma Rose couldn't see in the dark. "Why not?" Violet inquired.

"The storm," Grandma Rose said simply.

The quiver in her voice gone and now replaced with confident curiosity, Violet asked, "Have you ever counted them?"

It was a good answer: "No, because I would lose count. And because you can't count that high. And because I don't want to know how many stars there are. *That* is the mystery."

"Do you like mystery?" Violet wanted to know.

Grandma Rose gave a dreamy sigh. "I love mystery. Mystery is magic and imagination."

"Are you mystery and magic and imagination?" Violet had to know.

"I am," Grandma Rose smiled. "Are you?"

Shrugging in the dark, Violet told her, "Well, I like mystery and I believe in magic and Mama says I have a big imagination."

Smiling at the answer, Grandma Rose said, "Then you, Violet Graves, are mystery and magic and imagination."

The way in which Grandma Rose talked about life and the way she talked to people sent a warmth dancing all throughout their body. Violet experienced the joy Grandma Rose offered and she would be eternally grateful for that fact, forever grateful for that gift.

*****

Mama wasn't too angry with her daughter for leaving in the night like that. It seemed that her one and only concern regarding the matter was a fear that little Violet had disturbed Grandma Rose. Violet slept in that morning which Mama found odd. And so while Violet was sound asleep in her cozy little bed, Grandma Rose came to the Graves' house to explain to Mama Violet's disappearance in the night.

Mama didn't allow sleep-overs. It wasn't until Violet was older when she would find out Mama's reason. Mama especially didn't like the idea of Violet having a sleep-over at Grandma Rose's.

"Grandma Rose is old, Violet. She needs her rest," Mama decided.

"Bedtime is a waste of my time," then nine-year-old Violet had said.

Mama raised an eyebrow and shook a finger in light teasing. "Now you respect your elders, Little Miss Violet."

lessons

"So Grandma Rose, what is the lesson for today?"

Grandma Rose didn't look up from her hand-lettering activity. Grandma Rose was not the kind of grandma who would sew or knit or quilt in her free time. No, not Grandma Rose. "You were expecting a lesson?"

Violet shrugged, suddenly confused and unsure. "Well, you're always teaching me something."

Now it was Grandma Rose who shrugged. "Everyone teaches everyone something."

"See, Grandma Rose, there's an example of a lesson," Violet pointed out.

A chuckle. "Alright, then, my little flower. Do *you* have a lesson to teach me today?"

A giggle. "But don't you already know everything?"

Grandma Rose smiled good-naturedly. "Why would you think that?"

Violet was smiling shyly.

"Is it because I'm old? Or because I'm crazy?" Grandma Rose faked offense.

"I think it's both." There was no humor in Violet's voice; simple seriousness.

Then Violet asked of Grandma Rose, "Do you think we get crazy because we get old?"

Grandma Rose loved to laugh. "Oh Violet, Old Grandma Rose was born crazy. And that's how I'm going to die."

Violet pondered the thought. "Are we all born crazy?"

It was a good question. "I think so. Some are born crazier than others."

Violet pondered some more. "Do we all die crazy?"

Grandma Rose shook her head, a grave look shadowing her sunny face. "No. Some lose their crazy sometime during their life. They get sad, they get mad, they forget to be glad. They forget about their crazy."

"That's a good lesson," Violet approved.

Grandma Rose gave the conversation a pause, then said plainly, "Life is a lesson." Pause. "Violet, what will you learn?"

Violet's answer to that question would change often throughout her life.

a little crazy

"Violet?"

"Yeah?" Violet smiled back at that famous Grandma Rose smile.

The quirky pair were sitting on giant pillow cushions on the floor of the living room. Violet's was bright red and Grandma Rose's was dark purple. The activities for the day were meditation and conversation. Meditation was Grandma Rose's choice; conversation was a shared idea, as always.

"Tell me something. And be honest with me."

Violet would try. "Okay. I'll try."

Grandma Rose chuckled and her eyes were laughing also. "Tell me, Violet, is my house too crazy?"

"Do you mean good crazy or bad crazy?" Violet wanted clarification.

Grandma Rose posed a question: "Well, Violet, do you think crazy is good or bad?"

"It can be good…" Violet supposed.

Grandma Rose pointed a finger towards the dusty bookshelf going along the hallway. The fingernail that belonged to the pointing finger was painted yellow. None of her fingernails on either hand matched; each nail was its own color. "Grab that dictionary, Violet, would you?"

Violet fetched the old book. Her young-person hands didn't match well with the ancientness of the book. The dictionary oozed experience and stories; it was an old book, and its content – words – came from experiences and perspectives. Violet, on the other hand, lacked both experience *and* stories. And then there was Grandma Rose. Who was an amazing story herself.

Grandma Rose gave Violet a homework assignment to work on. "I want you to look up… the words… hmm, let's see… how about… *weird*… and… *beautiful*."

Soon Violet learned the exact definitions of the two words.

An excited Grandma Rose pressed, "So me and my house… Weird? Or beautiful?

It was hard to decide. "Maybe… weirdly beautiful?"

Violet never heard Grandma Rose whistle. "Ah. Smart girl. *Weirdly* beautiful. Combine the strange with the lovely and the lovely with the strange. That's what life does to us."

A long silence entered the air between them as the two women, one old and the other young, pondered by themselves.

Then the silence hesitantly dismissed itself.

"Weirdly beautiful," Violet pondered. "It's a crazy kind of beautiful."

"Life," Grandma Rose added.

Violet would add that on her daily to-do list from that day forward – that is, to always try and see life as beautiful, even and especially during the times when it seemed not so beautiful.

And she did see it as such.

laughing

"How was your day?" Violet asked politely.

There was a shrug before the response, "I did nothing today."

Grandma Rose doing nothing? Very shocked and a little perplexed, Violet clarified, *"Nothing?"*

Laughing, Grandma Rose said, "Nothing but laugh."

The comment made Violet laugh. Everyone laughed when Grandma Rose was around.

Violet had a question for Grandma Rose. "Do you laugh when you're alone?"

"I laugh the loudest when I'm alone," Grandma Rose said proudly.

Violet had another question. "Do you talk when you're alone?"

"I talk the most when I'm alone," Grandma Rose said, again, with pride.

"Grandma Rose, you're silly," Violet decided.

Grandma Rose took it as the greatest of compliments. "I'm a lot of things. And I'm glad that silly is one of them."

Then Grandma Rose was making funny faces. Her beautiful old-person face was transformed into many different masks with many different personalities. Violet was more than amused and her laughter only increased Grandma Rose's mad humor; the funny faces just got worse and worse.

Once the laughter between them subsided, Grandma Rose's original, beautiful, old-person face was back.

Then the old-person face was awfully serious. "I want to teach you something," Grandma Rose said plainly.

"Teach me what?" Violet inquired.

"Sometimes it will be hard to find something to be happy about. Sometimes you'll feel sad. Sometimes it will feel like things in your life want you to be sad. But you shouldn't hold back the laughter and the smiles and your happiness. It's there inside. Sometimes very deep inside, hiding under all the sad things."

"What if I think about my daddy? That's sad." Violet's fear and sadness leaked into the air.

Grandma Rose was quiet for just a moment, thinking thoughtfully. "Yes, that is sad," she said, paused, then went on, "I had a good daddy, so I don't know how it feels to feel sad when you think about your daddy." The pause seemed much longer this time. "But I would say to think about your mama. How she loves you and how she is there for you. Your mama is your friend. She is always there."

*****

When Violet returned home, Mama was there. She was there for a hug hello. She was there for an "I love you" kiss on the forehead. Mama was there.

Violet couldn't stop smiling for the rest of the day. She was thinking about the latest thing Grandma Rose had said.

getting brave

Today was one of the few days where *Grandma Rose* came over to *Violet's* house.

A tired Violet answered the door upon hearing the three happy knocks.

"Let's you and me go for a walk today, Violet," Grandma Rose decided decisively.

Violet squinted her eyes in confusion. "Grandma Rose, I think you forgot."

Grandma Rose didn't say anything; she just smiled. And her smile said everything.

"Grandma Rose, don't you remember that I'm currently a cripple? An invalid?"

Tomorrow marked the two-week anniversary of how Violet became a temporary cripple, an invalid.

The fact didn't seem to faze Grandma Rose; she just continued that Grandma Rose smile. Then she turned to point at something behind her. Violet stretched her neck to the left so she could look at whatever it was that had Grandma Rose so excited.

Sitting and waiting on the front lawn was a wheelchair. Violet wrinkled her little freckled nose. *That's for old people,* she thought, slightly offended.

Violet tried with all her might not to sound rude or annoyed. "Where did this come from?"

The smile didn't go away. "Oh, Grandma Rose finds all kinds of things. She's been around a long time. She knows where to find the best things."

"You're being mysterious again," Violet disapproved teasingly. "But I really wish you didn't get me this wheelchair."

"I didn't get it for you," Grandma Rose said quickly. "I am letting you borrow it before *you* give it away to someone *else*."

"But, Grandma Rose," Violet sighed dramatically. "I don't know any other girls my age who broke their leg because they jumped over a fence trying to impress a cute boy at school."

"Oh you'll think of someone. Or you'll see them. And that's when you'll know that you need to be of service."

And so the day went.

Violet got permission from Mama to hang out with Grandma Rose for the day. Grandma Rose pushed Violet around in that little, old-people wheelchair. They went to the park where they fed the birds. They went to the store where they bought and ate candy. They went to the dog park to count all the yellow dogs. And that was their day. Another day full of quiet, little things. The only difference between this day and all the others was – in Violet's eyes – today was a day to get brave. Violet was the kind of girl who blushed easily, who stuttered when put on the spot. To be in a wheelchair for a day was highly embarrassing to the poor girl. But she did it. And she did it for another person – not just herself. She took an attention-grabbing ride in a wheelchair, doing all kinds of fun stuff with a crazy old lady, so that this wheelchair would get some good luck and happy memories for the next person.

*****

Two weeks after that day, Violet found the perfect spot to leave the wheelchair. She left it outside of a trampoline park. She thought that someone would need it. Someone would need it. And Violet would never find out the story.

not today

"Oh hello, Violet," Grandma Rose said sleepily upon opening the door and seeing the pajama-wearing girl.

"Hi, Grandma Rose." Violet then noticed the tired eyes, so unlike Grandma Rose.

"I'm not feeling so well today," Grandma Rose said, "Why don't you come back tomorrow? Does that sound good?"

"Are you okay?" Violet's mind flashed to scenes of her dying grandparents, one by one.

The old woman nodded her head, then shook her head. "Grandma Rose is just tired today. Sometimes it's a lot of hard work to be a human."

Violet nodded her agreement, hugged Grandma Rose bye for now, and was about to head home when –

"Oh and Violet?" Grandma Rose stopped her.

Violet hurriedly turned around to face her. "Yes, Grandma Rose?"

Grandma Rose's happy smile didn't match the sadness in her eyes. "There is no such thing as a bad day."

Violet said "Okay" with a smile, then headed for her house across the street. Her smile didn't last too long though – because of thoughts that beautiful Grandma Rose wouldn't last forever. One day she would wilt.

wise woman

"A wise woman once said to stop and smell the roses."

"Who said that?" Violet had to know.

Grandma Rose smiled a sad smile before she told her. "My mama did. A long time ago. But my mama wasn't the one who started that philosophy. Someone else came up with the quote: Stop and smell the roses."

There was a pause and in it was Violet's admiration for Grandma Rose.

The pause ended with Grandma Rose's sudden words, "Do you know why my name is Rose?"

"You mean *Grandma* Rose?" Violet was teasing.

Grandma Rose's eyes matched the humor in Violet's voice; her eyes were laughing. "A baby cannot be born a grandma. Our names change all throughout our lives."

Another small silence and then, "But do you know why my name is Rose?"

Violet tilted her head and blinked her butterfly eyelashes. "Because your mama knew you'd be pretty as a rose all your life?"

A light laugh. "You are wise, too, Miss Violet."

Grandma Rose's eyes were still smiling – it was a sad thing when they were not – and Violet's freckled cheeks were just starting to blush again even though they just recently recovered.

Grandma Rose corrected Violet's idea, "But no, no, Violet. I was named Rose because of that motto my mama lived by."

"To stop and smell the roses?" Violet said in that sweet voice.

"To stop and smell the roses," Grandma Rose confirmed.

After a slight and thoughtful pause, Violet asked, "But what does it mean?"

Grandma Rose's thoughtful response: "There is good in the day and we should acknowledge it and thank it." It was her greatest therapeutic voice.

"What is the good in today?" inquisitive Violet inquired.

Without a moment's hesitation: "Me teaching you this motto that will probably save your life."

"Am I going to die?" Violet's voice was an interesting mixture of curiosity, sarcasm, and fear.

Grandma Rose addressed each of Violet's current emotions. "Everyone dies. But no, Violet, you have a long life. And it's going to be beautiful. Very beautiful."

"How do you know?" Violet wanted to know.

Grandma Rose was almost… *smirking?* "Because in another life I was a fortune-teller."

"And you still have the powers?" False incredulousness in the girl's voice.

Grandma Rose laughed first, then Violet's little laugh came next.

fake cupcakes

"Oh. Hello, Violet." The almost-always-cheery voice was now dreary.

Experiencing an immediate wave of concern and confusion, Violet frowned deeply at the tone.

The woman said, "I'm not feeling well."

"Again?" Violet's voice was a violent combination of sadness and anxiety.

Then there was a light shining and growing in Grandma Rose's eyes. "I need to rephrase that. I'm not feeling *myself*."

Violet looked hard into Grandma Rose's eyes, trying and failing to understand.

When Grandma Rose got her smile back, she said, "I have an idea. Let's you and me have ourselves a happy little picnic right here on the floor."

Violet's eyes went down to look at the picnic basket she was holding.

"Oh! Heavens, how beautiful. It would seem that you, Miss Violet, were thinking about a living room picnic as well." There was an exaggerated wink at the end of Grandma Rose's sentence.

Violet was a fast learner and, shortly after meeting Grandma Rose, she realized that you just simply went with things when you were around Grandma Rose. She held out the pink picnic basket for Grandma Rose to take.

But it wasn't just any ordinary picnic. There was no *ordinary* in Grandma Rose's house – both on Grandma Rose's part as well as her interesting, creative guests. It seemed that Grandma Rose attracted a unique crowd. Violet brought a little plastic cupcake alongside the edible food. The plastic cupcake probably looked more delicious than the peanut-butter-and-jelly sandwiches so obviously made by the hands of a nine-year-old.

So the unordinary picnic involved a little girl bringing a fake cupcake. The unordinary picnic also involved a silly game to go with the fake cupcake.

"Violet," Grandma Rose said softly. "What are the fake cupcakes in your life?"

"What do you mean?" Violet asked, interested.

"I mean," Grandma Rose went on to say. "What are the things in your life that seem real or true, but couldn't be further from the truth?"

Tilting her head, the frown was back. "Do you have an example?" Violet fished.

After a chuckle, Grandma Rose had an example. "For me, it seems that I should feel lonely living alone. But it's not true. I have me, myself, and I. And I have a nice little girl named Violet who sometimes comes to hang out with me."

Now the young lady was smiling. "Oh. I think I'll like this game," Violet gushed. She said the words with awe and respect.

But soon she was frowning. It was a deep frown and it was one that looked like it would never smile again. One thought destroyed the fun in the game.

"It seems that my daddy doesn't love me."

There were two quivering lips in the room.

"Is that true?" Violet's blue-mood voice begged for the answer. "Or is that a fake cupcake?"

Grandma Rose took a deep breath and let it out slowly before she spoke to calm Violet's anxiety and worst fear. "I don't know if it's true and I don't know your father, so I can't say. But if you ever have a sad thought like that, think of who definitely does love you. Your mama. Your new puppy. Your friends. Your Grandpa Rex. Your dear old friend Grandma Rose. There are many, many people who love you, Violet. And the amazing thing is that there are many people who will never tell you that they love you."

Well, what was there to say to something like that? Violet could only smile and tear up.

Then came the words: "Another fake cupcake is that I'm not pretty…?"

Suddenly something in Grandma Rose's eyes looked painfully upset; they almost flashed. "Violet, will you please go into my bedroom and bring me the two lipsticks on my vanity?"

Violet nodded and smiled, always excited to be a helper. Her solemn demeanor was replaced with happiness now that she was needed.

"It's the second room on the right," Grandma Rose called out as Violet walked in the right direction.

Soon Violet was back with two lipsticks, their colors concealed by the black caps. Grandma Rose invited Violet to remove the cap of a random tube of lipstick.

"This one's purple," Violet announced.

"Would you like to try it on?" Grandma Rose offered.

Violet's eyes bulged in amazement at the question being asked of her.

Grandma Rose giggled girlishly. "Have you ever tried on makeup before?"

Violet frowned and shook her head. "Mama said that makeup isn't good enough for me. She says that I'm too pretty."

Grandma Rose giggled another girlish giggle. "Pucker up."

Once the lipstick was applied to Violet's lips, Grandma Rose invited her to investigate her new look in the vintage mirror hung on the wall in the hallway.

"It's like violets on my lips!" Indeed. It was *violet* purple. Very Violet.

Then it was Grandma Rose's turn to try on a lipstick. Hers was a different shade of purple; eggplant.

Grandma Rose asked Violet another favor, this time to bring her a napkin from the bizarre swan napkin holder. It was bizarre because the napkins were supposed to make it look like it had feathers.

Grandma Rose slowly and delicately brought the napkin to her purple lips and planted a kiss on the once-clean napkin. Then she held it out towards Violet for her to take. Violet took it and gave a girlish giggle herself.

"Kisses from Grandma Rose. Kisses and loves and hugs for lovely, loving, loveable Violet."

dancing in the rain

Violet immediately found Grandma Rose upon entering the house after giving a knock and receiving a happy "come in."

Grandma Rose was sitting in one of her yellow table chairs and was smiling both mysteriously and mischievously. "Violet, tell me," Grandma Rose smiled bigger and so did her voice. "Is it raining?"

Violet shrugged. "It's sprinkling."

"Perfect," Grandma Rose's voice was delighted. "I prayed for sprinkling."

"Why?" Violet asked.

"Violet? Do you know what we're going to do?" Grandma Rose asked excitedly. Her expression was animated and very much alive, so unlike the average little old lady.

"What?" Violet asked.

"We – you and me – are going to go outside, run around the yard two times, and come back inside." The elderly woman was clearly not the most mature.

"Why?" Violet asked.

"Because God gave us rain and we should enjoy what God gives us," Grandma Rose answered matter-of-factly.

Violet asked the question, "But why two times?"

"Why run around the yard two times? Because only one time wouldn't be fun, and we would get soaking wet and get a cold if we go around more than twice." It was a funny answer.

*****

And so the pair ran around the yard two times. Both got soaking wet. Grandma Rose did not catch a cold, but Violet did.

crystal clear

Violet was too busy running around the yard last week to have noticed the intricate and very beautiful chandelier hanging from Grandma Rose's back patio. Today she noticed it, and admired it. Grandma Rose caught her stares. It was the week after their backyard run, the backyard run that got Violet sick with a cold. Violet was feeling a lot better now. You would think the memory of the run would have made her feel worse – because that was what technically got her sick with the cold; but, no, running in the rain, running in circles, running with crazy Grandma Rose, running for no apparent reason… it was enough to make anyone feel a little bit happier about life.

"Why do you have a chandelier outside?"

Grandma Rose took a sip of her chocolate milk; she was drinking chocolate milk out of a hot-pink-colored teacup. Then setting her drink aside, Grandma Rose admired the chandelier Violet wanted history on. From Violet's point of view, it looked like Grandma Rose's eyes were brighter and more brilliant than the chandelier. It seemed a long silence, and then…

"So you want to know the story of the chandelier," Grandma Rose prefaced.

"It has a story?" Violet was easily intrigued.

Grandma Rose smiled. It was a sad smile. "Everything and everyone has a story."

The lack of happiness in Grandma Rose's face was deeply bothering Violet, so she smiled a sincerely happy smile, hoping that it would be contagious. It was; Grandma Rose was soon beaming again.

"So," Grandma Rose began. "The story of the chandelier. It goes like this…"

Violet shifted in her chair, getting more comfortable on the chair cushion. *Story time with Grandma Rose,* she thought to herself, thrilled.

"Once upon a time…"

Pause.

"No, no, I don't like that."

Pause.

"Once there was…"

Pause.

"Yes, there, that's better."

Content sigh.

"Once there was a cute little thrift store called Thrifting at Theodore's. It was one of Little Rose's favorite places to go growing up. She first went there with her mama. Then she would go there alone as she got older. It was not 'cool' to go to the thrift store back then, so she didn't go to the thrift store with anyone her age nor did she tell anyone that she would sometimes go there. It was her little secret. She would find all kinds of things. Rose was very poor and so she rarely left the thrift store with anything. She was too poor to buy pretty things. But it was fun to look."

Pause.

"Grandma Rose needs a drink. Just a moment, Violet." Grandma Rose then took a drink out of the chocolate milk carton as if she had never had anything to drink before in her life. She gulped it down quicker than quick. Then, quicker than quick, she was back to her story. Then the story changed to first-person.

"Right, so. It was fun to look. And then one day… guess what I see? I see the prettiest thing! All sparkles and shine and happiness and prettiness – a chandelier! I knew at once that it was just the thing. My mama had been so sad for so long and her birthday would be soon. If she saw this chandelier, I knew she would smile."

Violet nodded her approval in her excitement.

"Boy, was I excited! This would be just the perfect thing for Mama. This was sure to cheer her up. Mama had been sick for a while now and she deserved a great birthday. She did a lot for me. She deserved it."

Pause.

"You want to know something pretty amazing about Thrifting at Theodore's?"

Violet blinked her big eyes.

"If an item doesn't sell after a while and once it starts to collect dust, they plop it outside by a sign that says FREE. And that's where I found the chandelier."

Pause.

"But it would seem that the shiny, happy chandelier got another person's attention, too."

Uh-oh, Violet's inner voice went, dismayed.

"I didn't see the man until I saw that the chandelier was gone. I was busy petting a stray cat that ran across the road. When I turned around from the cat, the precious chandelier was gone and a man was walking away from the thrift store. He was in a spotless suit and he was carefully carrying the precious chandelier. When I ran after him, he heard me and turned around and I saw that he had a kind face. I didn't beg, but I did ask him, 'I'll give you one penny for it.' And do you know what he said to me? That man immediately told me – no hesitation, no thought – he doesn't want my money. He said what he did want was for me to take the chandelier and do something good with it.

And I did. I gave it to my mama. Mama would die two years later.”

There was a beautiful stillness in the air, filled with emotion; silent, thoughtful. The minds of a little girl and an old lady thinking and pondering.

“This, Violet, was one of the very… most… *greatest* things that ever happened to me. This experience was an opportunity. This experience was a lesson. I learned from this experience, Violet, how important it is to help people, to love people, to give, to bless. Not many people were nice to my mama and me. We were among the poor class.”

There was that same reverence in the room. It was the reverence that came just before or just after Grandma Rose said something profound and thought-provoking. This happened often.

“Kindness is free, Violet. You cannot buy it, but you can give it. And you can receive it.”

“Wow,” Violet said in clear awe.

“Yes. Wow.” Grandma Rose smiled and the smile was followed by a wink.

Then Grandma Rose had a surprise. “I have something for you.”

It looked like a journal. Pretty and pink with a blue lace bow. It was pretty to look at and it made Violet smile.

There was an intense wonder and mystery in Grandma Rose's eyes that got Violet pondering. "And what's your story, Miss Violet?"

Now Grandma Rose's happiest of smiles was back.

happiest of birthdays

Mama had a one-on-one birthday party for her daughter, a mother-daughter date, just the two of them. Violet made it perfectly clear that she was "much too shy for the company of a bunch of crazy, loud, obnoxious girl friends." And so there were two birthday parties for Violet that year – one just her and Mama and the other her and Grandma Rose. She was now at Grandma Rose's house.

Violet removed the gift from its spot inside the box. "It's a sock…"

"Happy Birthday, Violet!" Grandma Rose exclaimed.

Violet examined the sock, a lime-green color with purple toe and heel and its pattern blue snowflakes, orange leaves, and yellow flowers. "But it's *one* sock," Violet stressed.

"Yes, I can count," Grandma Rose laughed out.

After the opening of the present containing one sock, there was chocolate cake along with chocolate milk and chocolate ice-cream. The happy pair sang songs together and had a dance party. Grandma Rose planned a really fun activity – dress up! The evening was recorded on a cheap video camera so as to always remember this birthday party. Violet would look back on this day and watch the video every single one of her birthdays for the rest of her life.

It was one of the happiest birthdays Violet would enjoy. And it included one single sock. That following Christmas would include the other sock. Lime-green. Purple toe and heel. Its pattern blue snowflakes, orange leaves, and yellow flowers.

homeless heart

"Grandma Rose, I have a question," Violet posed.

"What is your question?" Grandma Rose asked.

And now it seemed that Violet didn't want to ask after all. "Well…"

Gently, Grandma Rose prodded. "Well, what? You know you can always tell or ask Grandma Rose anything, Miss Violet."

Then it came out in a burst: "Have you ever met a hobo?"

Grandma Rose was silent for a moment; it was a dreadful silence. "I have met homeless people, but never a hobo."

This confused Violet. "Aren't they the same?"

The frown told Violet they were not. "*Hobo* is not a very nice word to describe a person."

"Oh. I'm sorry." And Violet was sorry; she wanted to please Grandma Rose, and, much more importantly, she wanted to be a good and kind person. Like Mama taught her and Grandma Rose showed her.

The words were spoken bluntly, but with an underlying loving kindness. "Don't be sorry. You can use the word. I personally, however, would not, so I do not."

Because Grandma Rose did not, Violet did not want to either.

Grandma Rose could sense that the topic was something deeper to Violet. "But why do you ask?"

"Well, there is a… *homeless*… woman" – Violet emphasized the word to please Grandma Rose – "who my mama and me see at the grocery store sometimes."

"Oh?" Grandma Rose encouraged.

Violet's voice was blue. "Yeah. I feel bad for her."

It was a subtle urging: "If you feel bad for someone, I think the best way to feel better is to do something nice for them."

Now Violet's voice was warming. "Well, Mama gives her some of our groceries sometimes."

There was a pause. When Grandma Rose paused before she spoke, it was going to be good. And then she erupted: "I know what we could do!"

Violet laughed at the overjoyed excitement. "What?" she giggled.

Grandma Rose was bursting. "Let's go to the thrift store and find a pretty purse –"

Violet wasn't all laughs and smiles anymore; she was bewildered. "But Grandma Rose, she is homeless and poor, so why would she need a purse?"

Grandma Rose told her. "I will put a $100 bill inside the purse."

Violet's eyes bulged. She had never even *seen* a $100 bill.

Becoming half-serious, Grandma Rose said, "A woman feels very powerful when she has a purse." Then she winked.

*****

The purse was a simple design, far from designer. Its original price could not have been more than $15. Violet contributed $2 of her own to buy the purse and Grandma Rose happily took care of the rest.

Violet and Grandma Rose, the dynamic duo, would soon learn that the inexpensive purse and the $100 inside given to a homeless woman would help them change the world, one person at a time.

*****

Violet tried to memorize the scene unfolding before her eyes so that she could watch the memory like a TV later. Violet almost giggled, she was so excited. It seemed like Grandma Rose was even more excited than she was; childish and giggling girlishly for an elderly woman. Grandma Rose jokingly named herself and her sidekick – Violet – the Flower Girl Spies. But the Flower Girl Spies were not pretend spies, but real spies in real life. And they were going to find out what their good deed of the day would bring.

And there she was! She was the one with the pretty blonde hair. Today she was again wearing that same red and yellow flannel that Violet was used to. Her name was Anna; Violet named her Anna. Violet thought she looked like an Anna. Violet could still see the woman's face clearly even from the distance of several yards. Her expression included her usual shifting eyes and downturned mouth.

Violet watched intently, eyes switching from squinting eyes to wide-eyed eyes, trying to accurately inspect the scene before her.

Anna hurried to her cart she left outside by the wall while she was in the store. She always did this; Violet the spy was keeping track. It appeared that her only purchase today was apples. The woman plopped the plastic bag of red apples on her already-heavily-loaded cart. Then she lifted the bag, staring down at something.

The purse! She looked to her left, then did a paranoid double-take. She then did something that surprised Violet; she was soon holding the purse and walking back to the front doors of the store. Then something caught Anna's eye, and Violet's too. A little yellow piece of paper fell to the ground. It was the note. Grandma Rose and Violet thought to lay a little note on the purse. So that Anna would know it's her purse. *Hers.*

This is for you

Something else surprised Violet: when Anna started crying. The tears started upon opening the purse. The $100 bill greeted her and made her cry. Violet knew Anna was crying because she had seen Mama cry lots of times in the past. Even from far away, Violet could detect the slight shaking and the head bent down, trying to hide tears.

Then Anna did something that *really* surprised Violet…

The woman stretched out her arms and threw her head back. "Thank you!" the woman called out to no one.

Then she started doing a little dance. It made people smile and laugh as they passed by. These people would have probably turned up their nose in her direction (due to her state of appearance), but it was her obvious and contagious happiness that gave them those smiles. Content smiles. "Life is good" smiles.

Was the "thank you" to the direct giver of the gift? or to her Maker?

Violet would ponder on that curiosity many days of her life.

a bad hair day

Grandma Rose noticed right away. She was an observant woman.

"Violet, your hair," was all she said.

It came out in a great big huff: "I cut it off."

"Why did you cut it off?" Grandma Rose asked sweetly.

Violet's voice was bitter, sour. "The popular girls make fun of my hair."

There was a sigh before Grandma Rose said, "Did you know that I used to have red hair? Once upon a time."

The lump in Violet's throat threatened to make Violet cry, so she didn't use her voice and only shook her head.

Grandma Rose continued with questions. "Do you think your mama is pretty?"

"Mama is beautiful." Violet managed to say the words in awe.

"Your mama's hair is red," Grandma Rose pointed out the fact.

Violet realized that this was more than a corny, cheesy pep talk.

"Do you think *you* are pretty?" Grandma Rose wanted to know, *had* to know.

By now the lump in Violet's throat was so strong and powerful that Violet was forced to cry to try to get rid of it. "I don't like red-head Violet."

"You will learn to," Grandma Rose promised, then paused to think deeply before she continued, saying, "One thing that we are supposed to do on this earth is learn to like ourselves. To live with ourselves." She hesitated again before hoping, "Do you think you can do that?"

"I have to live with this hair?" Violet choked; she was choking on her now angry tears.

Grandma Rose gave a light shrug and a loving smile. "You could dye it if you want. Maybe when you're older and your mama wouldn't mind anymore."

Violet's mind was blurry like her vision from the tears – it was distracting – but she managed to ask the question, "Did you… did you like your red hair?"

"Of course I liked my red hair," Grandma Rose said quickly.

"Why? *How*?" Violet wanted to know, *had* to know.

"It was a part of me," Grandma Rose said. "Why should I not like myself?"

Violet finally burst. "I don't like myself."

"Oh Violet." Grandma Rose was hugging her, holding her while Violet gave up on trying to hold in the tears. "You do love yourself. I know you do. I know because I see that you choose to be happy and you choose to be kind and you choose to do good. You know who you are and you want to get to know yourself even better. People who like themselves act that way."

Violet blinked one long blink. She thought maybe if she didn't open her eyes, she would never cry again. But her eyes opened and she opened her quivering mouth to say, "Do you know why I came to see you?"

"Why did you come to see me?" Grandma Rose's voice was often sweet like this.

"Mama said to go talk to Grandma Rose about my hair after I cut it off," Violet explained matter-of-factly.

It was hard for good-humored Grandma Rose to not laugh at Violet's serious tone. "I'm glad you did," was what she said.

"Why do you think Mama said that?" Violet wondered. Any trace of sadness or despair has fled Violet's voice by now.

"Why do you think your mama said that?" Grandma Rose asked her instead.

Violet said the words without humor. "I don't know. I just know you always do what Mama says."

Grandma Rose thought it was safe to let herself laugh at that. But that laugh didn't last long; a thought was consuming her. She was growing worried because little Violet relied on her too much and everyone seemed to know it, including and especially Mama.

"Grandma Rose, what are we gonna do today?"

Grandma Rose said three words: "Notes of encouragement."

"What?" Violet didn't know the meaning.

Now Grandma Rose used other words to further explain: "Encouragement. Strength. Peace. Comfort. Joy. Contentment."

That wasn't helping Violet's confusion.

Grandma Rose smiled happily and explained with kindness, "Notes that will make people smile. That will make their hearts happy."

Still perplexed, Violet smiled nonetheless.

"Is your mama busy?" Grandma Rose certainly hoped not; this was important, vitally so.

"She's busy doing…" Violet paused and thought. "Nothing."

Grandma Rose chuckled, then said, "We'll want a ride."

"Where are we going?" Violet was especially curious. And excited.

There was enthusiasm and mystery dancing in Grandma Rose's bright eyes. "The park. The park attracts all kinds of people. Sad ones, happy ones. Some will need our notes of encouragement."

Violet's curiosity was turning to pondering.

"What are some nice things that you wish people would say to you?" Grandma Rose inquired.

Now Violet was really pondering. "Well, I know some mean things I wish people *wouldn't* say to me."

"What kind of things?" There was an unknown pain in Grandma Rose's eyes.

Violet's eyes glistened with too many feelings. "Mean things. They make fun of me. My smile and my laugh. Especially my hair. My clothes, too. And the way I talk."

"How do you talk?" Grandma Rose said it softly.

"I don't know," Violet's voice shrugged. "Something about my high, girl voice."

After a thoughtful sigh, Grandma Rose said, "I think you have a lovely voice. A sing-song, Snow White princess kind of voice. It's happy and smiley – if a voice can smile." Then the old friend smiled. "But you know what, Miss Violet?"

"What, Grandma Rose?"

Grandma Rose turned her fragile body so she could directly face the little girl, for effect. "It's not so much what you sound like when you talk. But it's the things you say when you talk." And then when Violet's only response was a blink and a quivering lip, Grandma Rose continued, "And it sounds to me like those mean bullying girls don't say nice things when they talk. They have ugly voices, not you."

Violet could still only blink, her mind racing to absorb Grandma Rose's words.

"So. Is your mama doing anything?" Grandma Rose smiled.

*****

Mama dropped off Violet and Grandma Rose at Bluebell Park. It was more garden than park. There was an old woman who passed away nine years ago who had it in her will that there be more flowers in the city's biggest park. And so there were. They called it Bluebell Park, but there were no bluebells. Not one. But there were clovers. Lots of clovers.

Grandma Rose inhaled and exhaled the fresh air. "What a beautiful day. A beautiful day to pass out some notes of encouragement."

Violet's interest in the topic was sure growing. "What does that mean? Notes of encouragement?"

"It means something fun!" Grandma Rose exclaimed.

"What kind of fun?" Violet asked.

"The kind of fun where we make people smile." That smile Grandma Rose had on her face was enough to make anyone smile.

Only, Violet wasn't smiling in return.

"Like, we'll make their day?" Violet presumed, trying to understand.

"Perhaps." Grandma Rose winked.

Violet sighed a great sigh. "How are we going to do that?"

It was said with pizzazz: "We write random notes to random people."

Violet sighed a second time, the suspense and anticipation exhausting her.

Grandma Rose retrieved something from her kangaroo-pouch pocket. "Read this one to me. What does it say?"

Violet said, quite matter-of-factly, "Well, didn't you write it? Don't you know what it says?"

Grandma Rose chuckled and that made Violet giggle. Finally.

Then Violet looked down at the pretty paper in her hands. "I have to read *all* this?"

"You *get* to read it," responded Grandma Rose. "Please read it aloud, Violet."

"Okay."

Grandma Rose waited, her eyes sparkling and heart doing flips. She loved happy things. And notes of encouragement were probably one of the happiest things in all the world.

Hello, beautiful soul –

I wanted to write you this little note just because and without reason – without reason aside from wanting you to have a great rest of your day – and life.

You are a beautiful person with a beautiful heart and mind to match. You have gifts and talents close to magic. You bless others through your personality and light. Thank you for being you. All who have the great privilege to know you are blessed and so grateful for you. I love you and I hope you know you are loved by so very many.

Stay beautiful. And remember: You are a red, red rose.

Love,

a human who loves you

Violet didn't have any words to say after reading Grandma Rose's words drawn in beautiful handwriting.

"I have a job for you, Violet. A challenge."

Violet accepted Grandma Rose's challenge already.

"I challenge you to write three notes of encouragement for three unique strangers."

Violet asked the question, "How will I know a stranger is unique?"

"Oh, you'll know," Grandma Rose said airily.

Soon Violet was sitting at a green park bench, her mind blank and wordless. She sat and sat and thought and thought until she felt that nothing awestruck would happen. But suddenly, her pen started dancing in her fingers and she was writing, writing, writing.

Once the page was decorated with Violet's ten-year-old handwriting, Violet sat back content. That is, until a different feeling, one overwhelming and filled with dread, replaced the girl's contentment. "Can I copy this letter? And make two more notes?" she almost begged.

Grandma Rose greatly disapproved. "No, no. You are to be creative and meaningful and motivating. Every person is unique. Every note of encouragement should be unique as well."

Violet's mind went back to its blank state. But the fast-growing cobwebs in her mind soon disappeared when her imagination and kindness found the right words.

After two new letters befriended the first, Violet asked, "Do you want to read them, Grandma Rose?"

Grandma Rose had another "no" response: "No, I want these three letters to be between you and the people you give them to."

"But I read yours," Violet countered.

Now Grandma Rose had a "yes": "Ah, yes. I had you read mine because you needed an example."

"Speaking of example…" Violet mused.

"Yes?" Grandma Rose smiled.

"Mama says that you're a good example." Violet smiled at the words.

The complimented woman hardly blushed. "Your mama is very kind to say something like that."

Violet's voice squeaked, "Am I a good example?"

Grandma Rose had a swift mental answer for that.

"I want to be like you, Grandma Rose," Violet said in admiration of Grandma Rose.

There was to be another lesson in this moment, Grandma Rose decided. "To be an example means you inspire and influence – for good or for bad. And that's your choice, to choose to be an example for good, or for bad."

Violet had long ago decided. "I'll be good."

"Good choice."

Violet was expecting a wink or a smile. She got both – as well as a hug.

*****

It was an interesting afternoon. The first of Violet's letters was given to an elderly man with bad posture who blew Violet a thank-you kiss. The second letter was given to a quiet little boy walking his black lab puppy. And the letter Violet called "the grand finale" was given to a pregnant woman having a picnic by herself. The really interesting thing about the afternoon is that all three letters made all three people cry. Violet and Grandma Rose would never know that though.

weird names

"I got a goldfish and I named him Fluffy," Violet said with the utmost pride.

"What a cute name," Grandma Rose commented. "Why Fluffy?"

"Because it's something he is not." The girl's tone was matter-of-fact; it was funny when it was.

Grandma Rose loved the feeling of amusement. "And why would you want to name a fish something it's not?" she asked, trying not to laugh at the currently very serious Violet.

"To let him know that he can be whatever he wants to be," was the answer.

"Ah," Grandma Rose chuckled.

Violet lost her seriousness and giggled at the chuckle; a contagious sound.

Grandma Rose had a question for Violet: "If you could rename yourself, what would your name be?"

"Euphoria," Violet said without hesitation or thought.

Grandma Rose had to smile at that. "A beautiful word. A big word."

A serious look on her face, Violet told Grandma Rose, "I'm ten, but I know what it means." She paused, then defined it: "It basically means that you're very happy."

"And are you very happy?" Grandma Rose hoped.

Violet nodded and said, "I'm the happiest when I'm around you."

Grandma Rose's lips gave a smile, but her eyes looked sad. "Well, thank you, Violet. You make me happy as well."

"Happier than a pink penguin flying in cotton-candy skies!" Violet said in a laughing voice.

Both Violet and Grandma Rose had long ago learned that they did not make sense. They did not make sense individually. They did not make sense collectively. When the two were in the same room together, all sense left and in its place was nothing but nonsense. And that was where the magic was.

my heart is a garden

Violet plopped a pastel yellow rose in the empty vase sitting on Grandma Rose's dining table.

"Oh, how pretty," Grandma Rose breathed dreamily. "What is this for?"

"Just because," Violet said cutely.

"Just because?" Grandma Rose smiled. "I like 'just because.'"

A mixture of pride and shyness, Violet blushed.

Grandma Rose had a guess, but she wanted fact. "Why a rose?"

One shrug later, Violet said, "Roses make me think of you. I see them every time I go to the store and I always want to buy you one, but I don't have the money."

"How much did you spend on me?" Grandma Rose asked.

Violet shrugged another time. "This one was free."

There was a teasing smirk on Grandma Rose's lips. "Oh. Did Violet steal a rose today?"

"No!" Violet's expression was an expression of horror. Then she noticed the teasing in Grandma Rose's face. Now she recovered and could say, "There was a nice lady who said I could pick one for free." She added quickly, "She said she would let me if I gave it to someone."

"Well, thank you for making me that someone." Grandma Rose was honored. By a flower.

Violet was thrilled that Grandma Rose was so happy. She told her, "You always make my day every time I see you, Grandma Rose. So I wanted to make your day."

Grandma Rose beamed. "Violet, you are the kind of person who makes everyone's day. Everyone you come in contact with."

This time, Violet blushed from shyness and shyness alone.

*****

The following morning, Violet woke up to her mama's excited voice saying, "Violet, there is a surprise for you."

Violet rubbed at her sleepy eyes.

Mama's eyes were glistening. "It's outside. On the front porch."

The surprise had Violet's name written all over it – the front porch was covered in *violets*. It wasn't her birthday. It wasn't Christmas. It was just an everyday day. A random Saturday. And it was just because. And that was what made it so special.

There was a garden blooming in Violet's heart.

out of shape

It wasn't odd to Violet that the front door was wide open. Grandma Rose was so odd – a good odd, of course – that everything that would normally seem odd no longer was. "Grandma Rose?" she called.

"In… here!" Grandma Rose called out.

Violet followed the sound of the floral voice. When she discovered Grandma Rose, she couldn't laugh; it was too funny. "Grandma Rose, why are you running around in circles?" She paused, then listened closely. "And what kind of music is this?"

"I'm out of shape," Grandma Rose huffed. "And this is my running song," Grandma Rose puffed.

Violet was staring and laughing by now. Soon her eyes were watering and her face was turning red.

"Feel free to join in!" Grandma Rose invited her.

Somehow, between laughs, Violet was able to say, "I have exercise-induced asthma."

Grandma Rose's facial expression was almost grave. "I have… exercise-induced asthma… but I… don't let it… have me." Violet thought that Grandma Rose would wink after saying something like that. But the old lady didn't.

Grandma Rose had more to say. She stopped running and started walking. "Life is a run. You can't stop and walk. You have to hit that wall and get past it and run for miles and miles and run into the sun and feel the endorphins."

When Grandma Rose stopped talking, she stopped walking.

"You just said you can't stop and walk. And you stopped," Violet observed. Grandma Rose had taught her how to smirk; she was smirking teasingly now.

Grandma Rose managed a chuckle amongst the huffing and puffing. "It's symbolic, you silly goose."

Grandma Rose was always winking and it seemed like Violet was always rolling her eyes these days. But Violet quickly went from teasing to concerned when she noticed that Grandma Rose's panting worsened. And she was really *panting*.

"Grandma Rose? Grandma Rose! Are you okay?" Now Violet was gasping, too.

Now Grandma Rose was half-laughing and half-panting.

"It's not funny, Grandma Rose," Violet hmphed.

With eyes sparkling, Grandma Rose said, "Life is funny. To live it, you have to have some fun."

Life is for fun, Violet decided that day.

a broken heart

Years later and a very grave seventeen-year-old Violet sat on the couch, very unhappy. She wasn't pouting; she was sullen, solemn – depressed. It greatly bothered Grandma Rose to see her young friend in such a state that she didn't deserve.

"I didn't get asked to Prom," came the issue.

Grandma Rose's feelings changed in an instant. "What happened to Steven?" Grandma Rose asked blankly; her expression was blank and her voice unconcerned.

It came out quietly, "He broke up with me."

"And he broke your heart," Grandma Rose concluded.

"Yes," Violet's voice broke.

With a shake of her head, Grandma Rose said, "I would say I'm sorry, but I'm not."

Violet blinked, trying to blink away the tears fogging her vision so that she could read Grandma Rose's wrinkled face.

The old woman explained with the comment: "Steven was not a nice boy. You deserve better."

"But I liked Steven," Violet choked.

"I'm glad you did not love him," Grandma Rose said boldly. Everything she did and said was bold.

Now Violet's crying was slowing. Slowing because of understanding; because she was forced to think deeply and imaginatively in Grandma Rose's presence. Grandma Rose required two things: abrupt honesty and a little insanity.

Grandma Rose sighed. "A nice boy will find you. A nice boy will love you. You will be found and loved. Loved deeply and dearly."

"You promise?" Violet almost whimpered.

Shaking her head again, Grandma Rose told her, "I more than promise – I know."

Grandma Rose was wise. She was old with experiences and adventures. She lived through opportunity after opportunity. When she knew something, that something was real.

*****

Violet didn't get to enjoy her Senior Prom. She did, however, get to enjoy a different kind of Prom in a different kind of way. It was a fun and interesting night. Violet was still dressed in her Prom best; a lilac-purple dress, floor-length and ending in lace, sheer long sleeves decorated with sparse pearls and sequins. It was Violet's design and her mama's sewing skills that made the dress. However, the dress that made Violet feel like a princess was not what made the night truly enjoyable.

It was Grandma Rose. And Grandma Rose's house. The exterior of Grandma Rose's house included Christmas lights. Up all year. Always lit. Every night. Tonight, for Violet's Prom night, the interior, too, was decorated with a glow. All kinds of Christmas lights. Rainbow ones. Icicle ones. Golden ones. Flickering ones. All kinds. The lights were the highlight of Violet's night. Sure, the "dinner" (candy canes, cocoa, and mousse cake) was great. And of course the conversation cards throughout the "meal" were great. And then there was the activity – balloon painting – which was, again and of course, great. Thanks to an oversized t-shirt with a dachshund on it, Violet's dress was protected.

But it was all those lights. That's what made the night, the lights and especially Grandma Rose. And it wasn't just the physical glow and pretty twinkling of the lights. It was what Grandma Rose said to explain why all the lights.

"You are a light unto the world, Violet. There is a spark in your soul, Violet. Never forget it and never let it die out. Never let it burn out. If you let your light die out, you can't share who you are with the world. And the world needs you. The world needs Violet. Yes, the world needs more Violets."

What was the world going to do without Grandma Rose when the irreplaceable – and crazy – little old lady left this earth for heaven?

don't cry

"Grandma Rose." The eighteen-year-old girl's voice was shaky and sorrowful. You could go as far as to say *grief-stricken*.

Grandma Rose's eyes have seen a lot and she didn't like what she was seeing now; her eyes hated seeing her precious Violet so solemn and distressed.

"I'm so sad that I can't even cry."

This was one of those few times when Grandma Rose didn't know what to do or even what to say.

"I'm moving." The girl's tone was blank, bleak. "Mama is moving and I'm going away to college."

Now the words came. "Oh but Violet." She was trying not to lie; she had a false and lying smile both in her eyes and on her lips. "Moving is an adventure. Because of your move here, you were able to meet me and look what happened."

Now Violet was able to cry.

"We became very good friends," Grandma Rose offered.

Then Violet was able to cry harder. Acting like Violet's grandmother, Grandma Rose scooped up Violet – who was petite for her young adult age – in her shaky, fragile arms and sat her on her little lap. With a shaky hand to match her shaky arms, Grandma Rose softly pet Violet's red hair after collecting the tears running down the girl's freckled face.

Together they were two sad flowers.

my heart's breaking

It wasn't a dream that woke Violet that morning two years later. It was a nightmare. It started as a dream. But most dreams change.

Violet was back to her young self again. She was enjoying yet another afternoon with Grandma Rose. Until she wasn't anymore.

Grandma Rose and Violet were cutting out a zillion paper hearts for Valentine's Day. Of all colors and sizes. They would heart-attack the neighbors; they would stick a bunch of paper hearts on the doors in their neighborhood. But as Violet was gathering up all the hearts they created, they were tearing in the middle. Not by Violet's hand, or Grandma Rose's. No, they were tearing themselves straight down the middle of the heart. Broken hearts. Then another heart was being destroyed – Grandma Rose's. In the dream-nightmare, she died of a heart-attack right before Violet's eyes, among all the other broken paper hearts.

Violet said the words aloud in a shaky and stressed voice. "I need to see Grandma Rose. As soon as possible."

I love to see you

It's been two years and eleven days since Violet and Grandma Rose last saw each other. But who's counting? Well, Violet and Grandma Rose.

"I feel shy and awkward all of a sudden. Is that okay?" Violet said awkwardly.

Grandma Rose's wink was back. "I feel very excited to see you. Is that okay?"

Then and there the conversation flowed. Grandma Rose's smile and laugh and way of talking calmed Violet's anxiety. Violet was so glad to be able to tell Grandma Rose things again, this time things like college life – cramming for tests and pulling all-nighters, dorm drama and mean girls, cute guys and dating jerks, dealing with social anxiety and overcoming shyness. The good and the bad. Grandma Rose did a lot of listening and nodding. She did a lot of either happy-smiling or worried-frowning. Grandma Rose also did a lot of laughing.

On her long drive back to her college life, Violet found herself saying the words, "She's crazy. Crazy is good. At least the way she does it."

exciting news

One year later…

"Grandma Rose?" Violet's voice sounded at the open front door.

The crazy old lady was found dancing alone in her bright kitchen.

"Grandma Rose? I have some exciting news." The way Violet was beaming made her look even more stunning.

"Tell me this exciting news, Violet." Still swaying to the nonexistent music.

"I'm getting married!" Violet sang.

The dancing ceased just then. "To that nice young man you had me meet?" Grandma Rose clarified.

Violet smiled. "Yes, Vance."

Grandma Rose's voice was sad. "Oh, that's too bad."

Violet's beaming smile was quickly slipping. "I thought you liked him."

"Oh but I do," Grandma Rose said quickly. "He just doesn't deserve you. No boy does."

"But you're happy for me?" Violet hoped.

"I am delighted for you, Violet."

Hearing those words – and words coming from her favorite person – made Violet smile the biggest smile she has ever smiled.

more exciting news

Violet didn't like surprises, but she loved to give them. She didn't call Grandma Rose prior to her stopping in. She just stopped in.

"Grandma Rose? I have some exciting news," a beaming Violet said.

"Those were the exact words that you used when you told me you were getting married last year."

Violet was laughing. Her laughter was accompanied by tears. Happy tears. Euphoric tears.

"You don't have to tell me. I know."

The light, elated laughter dwindled, then ceased. Violet's tears had turned to real crying and her crying became more pronounced.

"You're pregnant."

Violet couldn't talk through the tears; her crying talked for her. She reached into her bag and pulled out the cutest pair of Converse shoes; they were newborn sizes.

"Congratulations, Violet. Congratulations times infinity." The words were said with such sweetness and kindness and admiration and adoration.

There was more: "I have something for you. It's under the tree."

Violet smiled and blushed at the surprise.

"It's been under the tree for a long time," Grandma Rose explained briefly.

Violet didn't ask the timeline for exactly just how long the gift had been waiting for her under the all-year-round Christmas tree. That was a part of the surprise, Violet assumed.

It was a sock, one lone sock. But not just any sock. It was a perfect sock for a newborn baby, tiny and cute. Oddly enough, it resembled that of Violet's sock. Its "match" was currently on Violet's left foot, underneath a yellow Converse shoe. Remember: Grandma Rose's joke was to give one sock for a birthday and the other matching sock for a Christmas.

Violet had no words for Grandma Rose; she could only laugh uncontrollably, tears gone.

There was more still: "There is something else for Baby as well."

It was a darling little baby's dress. It was decorated with embroidery – animals of all kinds, a zoo alive and breathing on a little article of clothing. The dress was a crisp white and the animals were stitched in silver and gold.

"May your sweet baby girl be as ferocious as a lion and as gentle as a lamb."

How Grandma Rose knew that Violet's baby was a girl, only God knew.

talking dogs

"Violet, I have been meaning to ask you something."

"Sure, anything, Grandma Rose."

The pair were making oatmeal cookies in Grandma Rose's kitchen. Violet's baby belly seemed to be in the way a lot.

There was a pause. Grandma Rose was the type of person who seemed to always have something to say and was never afraid or hesitant to say it. This conversation, she dreaded the words. "I have been stalling. I don't really want to ask."

"Is everything okay?" Violet was concerned now.

"Yes, yes, everything's fine." Then the aging woman sighed. The sigh didn't sound fine. "I just need a new home for my babies."

"Daxton and Daxton?" Violet's voice was higher, more emotional.

Forcing a smile – something the woman had some amount of experience with – Grandma Rose said, "Yes, Daxton and Daxton need a new home. Old Grandma Rose is getting too old to care for little doggies. Even if she is a crazy old dog lady."

Violet was careful not to sound as overly emotional as she felt. "I'll take them. If you promise to be my baby girl's godmother."

A grateful smile later, then, "That is a promise that I can keep."

That smile was sincere.

birthday blues

Violet once again invited herself over. Grandma Rose was once again happy to see her.

"Happy day, happy day," Grandma Rose gushed, "Beautiful Violet's birthday today."

"Aww, thank you," Violet gushed back.

A smiling – more like beaming – Grandma Rose had her own birthday coming up. It would be on Friday the thirteenth this year. Grandma Rose – so full of innocent teasing and bubbly light-heartedness – has been joking about her quickly-approaching unlucky birthday. This fact saddened Violet to an uncomfortable degree; what would an unlucky birthday bring to a fragile old lady? Another Grandma Rose birthday meant she was aging and getting closer to leaving her for heaven. Grandma Rose would be turning ninety-seven.

Grandma Rose interrupted Violet's negative thinking when she suddenly gave a pat to Violet's eight-month-bump.

"Grandma Rose will be right back."

Violet watched the old woman move slowly from off her rocking chair to get whatever it was she wanted to get from her bedroom. The old woman walked with a tired, uneven posture. Sadness was in Violet's eyes, sadness was in her thoughts. Grandma Rose had to see another birthday. Grandma Rose had to meet Violet's baby. Grandma Rose had to live. She wasn't allowed to die. The world would die without her. Violet was lightly crying and looking down at her folded hands when Grandma Rose returned back to her rocker. Violet had been in such deep thought that she hadn't even noticed Grandma Rose's return.

"Oh Violet, Violet," Grandma Rose cooed. "I don't know why you're crying, but I think I know. I won't say it because I don't want to make it more real for you than you already believe it to be."

Violet blinked back a single tear and swallowed out of anxiety and depression.

"I love you, Grandma Rose."

"And I love you, my little Violet flower."

Grandma Rose smiled, then gave another little pat to Violet's bulging belly. She then went to her rocking chair where she leaned her head back, rocking herself in the old, creaky rocking chair. Her eyes were closed and her breathing quiet and steady. Violet was struggling, trying to keep her tears nonexistent. It was time for her to go for the day. It was time for Grandma Rose to have a little rest. Violet got up from her cozy spot on the couch and waddled over to Grandma Rose where she planted a kind kiss on the

old woman's forehead. Violet gave another "I love you."
Either Grandma Rose did not hear the three words or she
already fell fast asleep, as she did not stir or say anything
back. The rocking had stopped.

*****

On Violet's way home, she cried. They were very
loud tears. When she got home, she sat in her red rocking
chair trying to ignore the now-angry tears.

a motto

Grandma Rose believes that there is no such thing as a bad day. She lives and breathes her motto. She radiates happiness and positivity. She looks at life with optimism and excitement, so much so that some find her close to insanity. Is it insane to be happy when there is seemingly nothing to be happy about? When there is such an empty sadness deep within the interior of your mind. When your life is an ugly domino effect of sorrow, pain, and negativity. When you have no power or control to change those blue, blue feelings. When happiness is seemingly impossible and so very odd…

But she chose happiness. Happiness didn't choose her. There was a natural high within Grandma Rose's mind, heart, and soul. No one but Grandma Rose and her doctor knew about the depression. It wasn't that it was a secret. It's wasn't kept quiet because of shame or fear. It wasn't to avoid attention or concern. Grandma Rose just didn't see it as something to be talked about. She didn't want to give the depression any more attention than it was already taking. The major depression's one wish was to kidnap Grandma Rose's happiness. Forever. But Grandma Rose fought it every single day with smiles and laughter, jokes and teasing, play and fun. Some days were made up of sincere joy, others false smiles.

Today was not a bad day. It wasn't that. Those days don't exist. But it was a hard day, a tough day. Grandma Rose felt tougher than the depression, but not today. Today was different. It was uncomfortable. She went to bed with a strong impression in her heart that she would never feel this way again.

roses are red

Violet examined the little picnic basket and its contents with a critical eye and a big smile. She and her mama had brought cookies when they introduced themselves to Grandma Rose. Now Violet was bringing Grandma Rose cookies when she introduced her baby. The cookies sitting in the middle of the picnic basket were surrounded by little notes, each note containing a single word that Violet thought described Grandma Rose. To name a few of Grandma Rose's descriptions: friend; family; beautiful; lovely; timeless; wise; real; raw; flower. Then the phone on the kitchen counter began vibrating, anxious to bring news as soon as it was answered. Violet answered.

"Hello?"

There was an awkward moment's silence, then a woman's voice, "This is Mrs. Summers?"

Violet Summers blinked. "This is her. Can I ask who's calling?"

"Nurse Angela," the voice said.

"Oh. Hello, Angela. How are you?" Only Violet wanted to know how someone *else* was doing; she supposed that Nurse Angela was fine.

There was a pause, then an odd sound broke the silence. One choked sob? "Things are okay. How are you?"

Violet paused, nervous. "I am well. Life is good."

"Good, good. I'm glad." She didn't sound glad.

Now Violet made that same one choked sob sound. "This is about Grandma Rose, isn't it?"

There was a deep, sad sigh on the other end.

"She died?" Violet knew.

Nurse Angela sniffed. "This morning."

Violet's eyes were closed, pushing back unwanted tears. "Thank you for letting me know."

"I wanted you to be the first to know." Quiet crying. Nurse Angela couldn't keep her professional character very well.

Violet knew that she should prepare for violent mourning.

"Can you please meet me at her home in a half-hour?" Nurse Angela said in a rush.

"I'll be there," Violet managed, then slowly hung up the phone.

*****

Slow-motion or quickly, Violet didn't know; she sloppily grabbed her polka-dot purse and Converse shoes. Violet swiftly but softly shut the lime green front door behind her. A purple Converse shoe on her left foot and a blue Converse shoe on her right foot.

*****

After Nurse Angela struggled through light tears to say it was a heart-attack, she pointed towards the kitchen.

"She left something for you. It's on the table."

Violet's teary eyes blinked in the direction of the kitchen table.

Then Nurse Angela slowly shook her head, trying to smile. "The picnic table."

Once at the picnic table, Violet found it.

It was an unfinished note with a kind intent.

Roses are red

Violets are blue

I want to tell you

I love

And that was where it ended. You knew that it was *you*, but you also knew that it could be and mean so much more.

"Can I take this?" Violet choked out.

Nurse Angela nodded solemnly and smiled kindly. "She wanted you to."

Violet was smiling a sad smile. "I save all my cards and notes. This one will be my favorite."

That was when Violet accepted and received Nurse Angela's hug.

"I was going to come see her today," Violet choked between tears. "I was going to introduce her to my baby and tell her that I named my baby girl after her. Rose."

"Only, you don't call her *Grandma* Rose, right?" Nurse Angela teased.

Violet and Nurse Angela shared a laugh and one last hug, then Violet went home to hug her husband and kiss her Baby Rose.

roses and violets

Violet Summers wrote four copies of the following poem:

Roses are red

Violets are blue

You have a Grandma Rose and a Mama Violet

Who love, love you

The first copy was for her first day of first grade. The second was for the day she graduated college. The third was for her wedding day. And the fourth was for when she had her first child.

Baby Rose would grow and tilt her head in confusion when her mama read her the first note. She would grow older and smile the most content smile when she read the second note. She would grow up and cry like she wasn't grown up at all when she read the third note. She would be all grown and cry worse than a baby when she read the fourth and final note. Only, that fourth note was *not* the final note.

Violet's daughter Rose would write many notes of her own for her own daughters, Violet, Rose, and Blossom. The tradition would carry on and on and on. There would be many Roses in the family. They created their own garden. Passing notes and passing along happiness and joy.

There would be many writers in the family. And they were all named Rose. There would be the book *Violet Rose* by Rose Sky. There would be *Violet's Rose Garden* by Rose Meadow. And there would be many others. A book from every generation written by one of Violet Summers' descendants.

Each Rose lived a content, beautiful, magical life, inspired by the original Rose. Grandma Rose's mystery, magic, and imagination blessed and changed the lives of thousands.

Thank you for reading my story and for joining me in my last years of adventure and nonsense.

-Grandma Rose (a true crazy old lady)

www.ingramcontent.com/pod-product-compliance
Lightning Source LLC
Chambersburg PA
CBHW051427150726
48000CB00005B/1993